To Phoebe H and Amelia

First published 2004
Evans Brothers Limited
2A Portman Mansions
Chiltern St
London W1U 6NR

British Library Cataloguing in Publication Data
Robinson, Hilary, 1962-
Batty Betty's spells. - (Zig zags)
1. Magic - Juvenile fiction. 2. Children's Stories
I. Title
823. 9'14 [J]

ISBN 0237527952

Printed in China by WKT Company Limited

Series Editor: Louise John
Design: Robert Walster
Production: Jenny Mulvanny
Series Consultant: Gill Matthews

ZIG ZAG

Batty Betty's Spells

by Hilary Robinson

illustrated by Belinda Worsley

Evans

Batty Betty always found…

...she got her spells
mixed up.

6

So when she tried to mend
a plate, it turned into a...

cup!

Her very worst day of all
was when she blocked
the sink.

She cast a spell to sort it out and turned her black cat...

pink!

hee hee

13

Things did not get better
when she started
a spring clean.

15

The spell for this
went very wrong and
turned her pink cat...

Ah, she thought, I know a spell to make my messy bed.

But when she waved
her magic wand,
it turned her green cat...

red!

Betty mixed a magic spell to clean her bathroom pipes.

But oh dear me – her poor red cat was...

head to foot in
stripes!

Betty then gave up
on spells,
and took her
broom and mac.

She flies around the sky
at night…

29

... so her striped cat looks

black!

Why not try reading another ZigZag book?

Dinosaur Planet   ISBN: 0 237 52667 0
by David Orme and Fabiano Fiorin

Tall Tilly   ISBN: 0 237 52668 9
by Jillian Powell and Tim Archbold

Batty Betty's Spells   ISBN: 0 237 52669 7
by Hilary Robinson and Belinda Worsley

The Thirsty Moose   ISBN: 0 237 52666 2
by David Orme and Mike Gordon

The Clumsy Cow   ISBN: 0 237 52656 5
by Julia Moffatt and Lisa Williams

Open Wide!   ISBN: 0 237 52657 3
by Julia Moffatt and Anni Axworthy